Rain Forests

Heather C. Hudak

Wonder Books
An Imprint of The Child's World®
childsworld.com

Published by The Child's World®
800-599-READ • childsworld.com

Copyright © 2023 by The Child's World®
All Rights reserved. No part of this book may be reproduced or utilized in any form of by any means without written permission from the publisher.

Photography Credits
Photographs ©: Patryk Kosmider/Shutterstock Images, cover (jaguar), 1, 3 (jaguar), back cover; iStockphoto, cover (background), 3 (background); Shutterstock Images, 2, 4, 5, 6, 8, 12, 22; Antonin Vinter/Shutterstock Images, 7; Mats Lindberg/iStockphoto, 11; Matthieu Gallet/Shutterstock Images, 15; Patrick K. Campbell/Shutterstock Images, 16; Danita Delimont/Shutterstock Images, 19; Gustavo Frazao/Shutterstock Images, 20, 20–21

ISBN Information
9781503857964 (Reinforced Library Binding)
9781503860353 (Portable Document Format)
9781503861718 (Online Multi-user eBook)
9781503863071 (Electronic Publication)

LCCN 2021952450

Printed in the United States of America

ABOUT THE AUTHOR

Heather C. Hudak lives in the foothills of the Rocky Mountains. She has written hundreds of kids' books on all kinds of topics. When she is not writing, Hudak loves to travel. She has visited about 60 countries and many rain forest ecosystems all over the world, including in Costa Rica, Argentina, and Vietnam.

RAIN FORESTS

Contents

CHAPTER ONE
What Is a Rain Forest Ecosystem? 4

CHAPTER TWO
What Lives in Rain Forests? 6

CHAPTER THREE
Why Rain Forest Ecosystems Matter 20

Rain Forest Terrarium . . . 22

Glossary . . . 23

Find Out More . . . 24

Index . . . 24

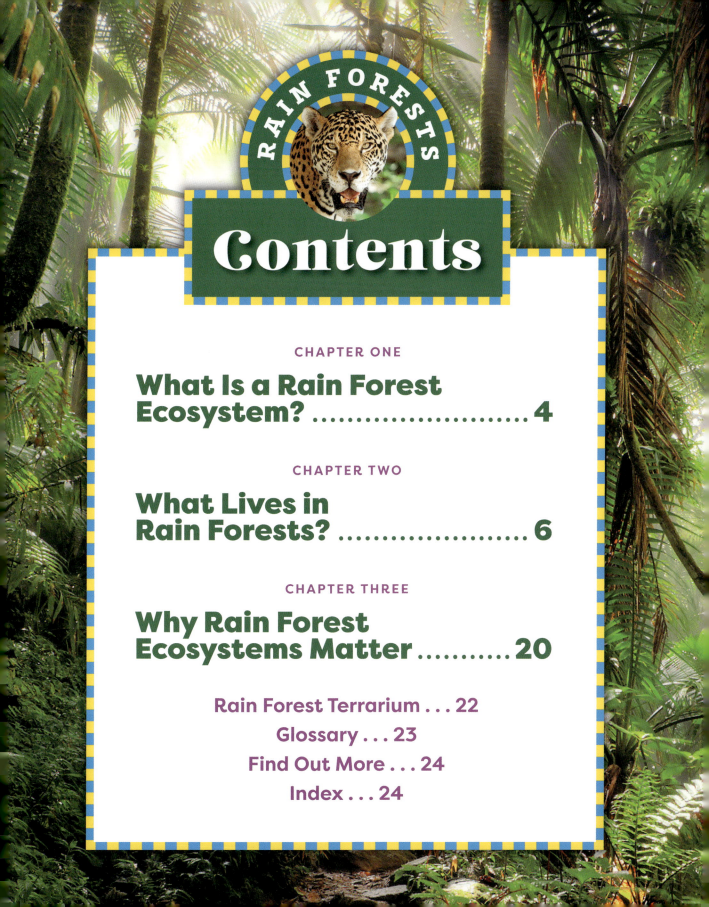

CHAPTER ONE

What Is a Rain Forest Ecosystem?

Rain forest **ecosystems** are thick jungles. They get a large amount of rain. There are two main types of rain forests. Tropical rain forests are found near the **equator**. They are hot and humid all year long.

Temperate rain forests are farther from the equator. They are not as hot or rainy as tropical rain forests. They have two seasons: a long, wet winter and a short, drier summer. Temperate rain forests are found in cooler places near coasts.

Rain forests cover less than 7 percent of Earth's surface. But they contain more than half of all plant and animal types.

LAYERS OF A RAIN FOREST

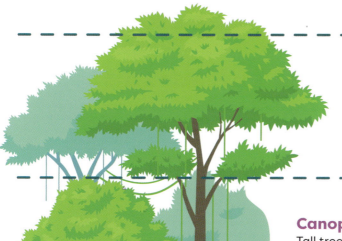

Emergent
The oldest and tallest trees tower above the canopy. Monkeys and birds are common here.

Canopy
Tall trees form a roof over the bottom layers. Up to 90 percent of rain forest plants and animals live here.

Understory
Young plants and trees are well protected from poor weather. They grow large leaves to reach the sunlight.

Floor
It is dark and humid here. The floor mainly consists of soil, **fungi**, insects, and bacteria.

CHAPTER TWO

What Lives in Rain Forests?

LEAFCUTTER ANTS

Leafcutter ants live on the rain forest floor. They dig underground nests. The ants use their jaws to tear apart plants. They carry plant pieces to their nests to make a garden. The garden grows a special fungus. The ants chew up plants and feed them to the fungus to help it grow. Then, the ants eat the fungus. The fungus and the ants depend on each other for survival.

Leafcutter ants use up more plant matter than any other group of animals in the rain forest. This helps make room for new plants to grow. The ants also turn over lots of soil when making their nests. This makes it easier for plants to grow.

There are 39 types of leafcutter ants.

DID YOU KNOW?

Leafcutter ants live in huge groups called colonies. A single colony can have as many as four million ants.

Wallace's flying frogs are also called parachute frogs.

WALLACE'S FLYING FROGS

Wallace's flying frogs live in the rain forest canopy. They do not really fly—they glide. Flying frogs use their strong back legs to launch off tall trees. They glide as far as 50 feet (15 m) through the air. The frogs have webbed feet and flaps of skin on their legs and arms. The flaps act as a parachute to keep the frogs from falling to the ground too fast.

Flying frogs are both **predators** and **prey**. They can glide in search of food or to escape being eaten. Tree snakes and other animals eat flying frogs. The frogs eat insects. By eating insects, the frogs keep the population from getting too large.

DID YOU KNOW?

Flying frogs have sticky pads on their feet to help them climb tall trees.

LONG-TAILED HERMIT HUMMINGBIRDS

Long-tailed hermit hummingbirds are **pollinators**. They live in tropical rain forests where there are many flowers. The hummingbirds use their long bills to sip **nectar** from flowers. Pollen falls on their heads as they rub against the flowers. The hummingbirds carry the pollen to other flowers. The flowers use the pollen to make seeds. Other animals eat the seeds and the new plants that grow from them.

Hummingbirds fly at speeds of 40 miles per hour (64 kmh). This burns a lot of energy. They need to drink a lot of nectar to keep going. Hummingbirds feed every ten to 15 minutes when they are active.

Long-tailed hermit hummingbirds have a white tip on their tail feathers.

Agoutis can weigh up to 13 pounds (6 kg).

AGOUTIS

Agoutis (uh-GOO-teez) are rodents. They live on the rain forest floor. They eat fruits, nuts, and seeds. Agoutis have very good hearing. They can hear ripe fruit falling off trees that are very far away. They also follow monkeys and pick up food the monkeys drop from trees. Agoutis bury food all over the forest to eat later. Sometimes, agoutis forget about the food they bury. The seeds and nuts grow into new trees and plants. Agoutis also spread seeds across the rain forest in their waste. Many plants and trees rely on agoutis to spread their seeds. Agoutis are also a source of food for predators. Eagles and jaguars eat agoutis.

DID YOU KNOW?

Agoutis are good jumpers. They can leap up to 6.5 feet (2 m) into the air.

SLOTHS

Sloths live high in the rain forest canopy. They have long legs and big claws to help them grip branches. They can eat, sleep, and give birth upside down in the trees. Sloths can barely move on the ground. They are in danger of attack from eagles, jaguars, and other predators. Sloths only come down once a week to get rid of their waste.

    Sloths are some of the slowest animals in the world. The leaves they eat do not give them much energy. Sloths are so slow that some types of algae grow on their fur. Algae are tiny plants. These algae are not found in any other place on Earth. The algae get water and shelter from the sloth's fur. They also make the sloth's fur green. This helps the sloth blend in with its surroundings.

Sloths do not have very good eyesight or hearing. They get around mostly by touch.

Some green anacondas can grow to be 30 feet (9 m) long. They can weigh 550 pounds (250 kg).

GREEN ANACONDAS

Green anacondas are top predators. They can hunt on land and in the water. These snakes have their eyes and nose on the tops of their heads. This helps them see and breathe while they swim. Anacondas are olive green with dark spots on the spine and sides. They blend in with plants and trees. It is hard for their prey to see them coming.

Anacondas squeeze their bodies around their prey to crush it. Then they swallow it whole. Anacondas eat just about any type of animal, such as deer, fish, turtles, and large birds. They keep prey animal populations from getting too large.

JAGUARS

Jaguars are some of the largest rain forest cats. Like other predators, they keep prey populations in check. This is important for rain forests' health. Jaguars mostly hunt at night. They search for food on the rain forest floor.

Jaguars have spots on their fur. This makes them hard to see. Prey cannot see the cats hiding in grasses, bushes, and trees. Jaguars also have padded feet so animals cannot hear them coming. Jaguars quietly follow their prey. Then they pounce on it. Jaguars are not fussy eaters. They will eat almost anything they can catch. Their diet includes frogs, armadillos, monkeys, deer, squirrels, snails, fish, turtles, rodents, birds, and many other animals.

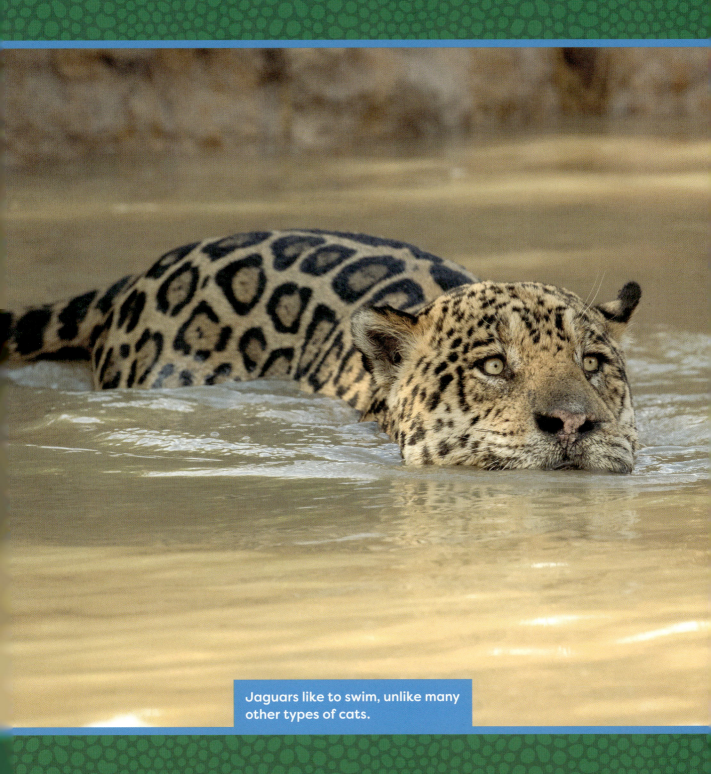

Jaguars like to swim, unlike many other types of cats.

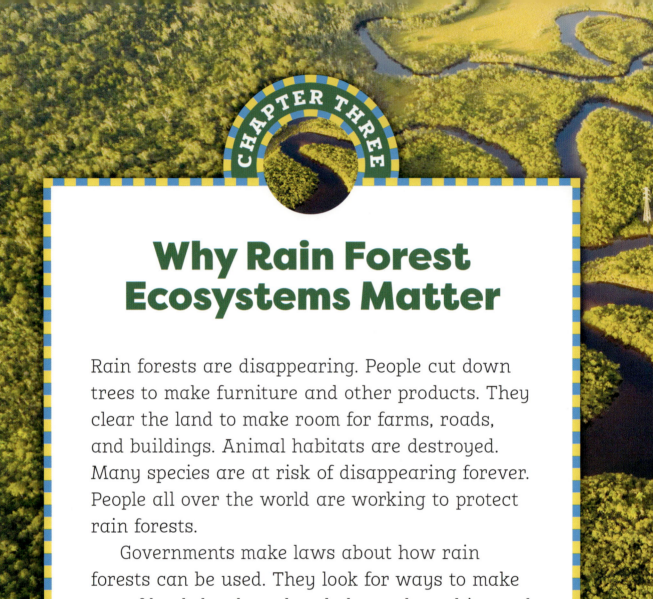

CHAPTER THREE

Why Rain Forest Ecosystems Matter

Rain forests are disappearing. People cut down trees to make furniture and other products. They clear the land to make room for farms, roads, and buildings. Animal habitats are destroyed. Many species are at risk of disappearing forever. People all over the world are working to protect rain forests.

Governments make laws about how rain forests can be used. They look for ways to make use of land that has already been cleared instead of cutting down more trees. Local farmers learn new farming methods to make the best use of the land. Organizations educate tourists about environmentally friendly ways to visit rain forests.

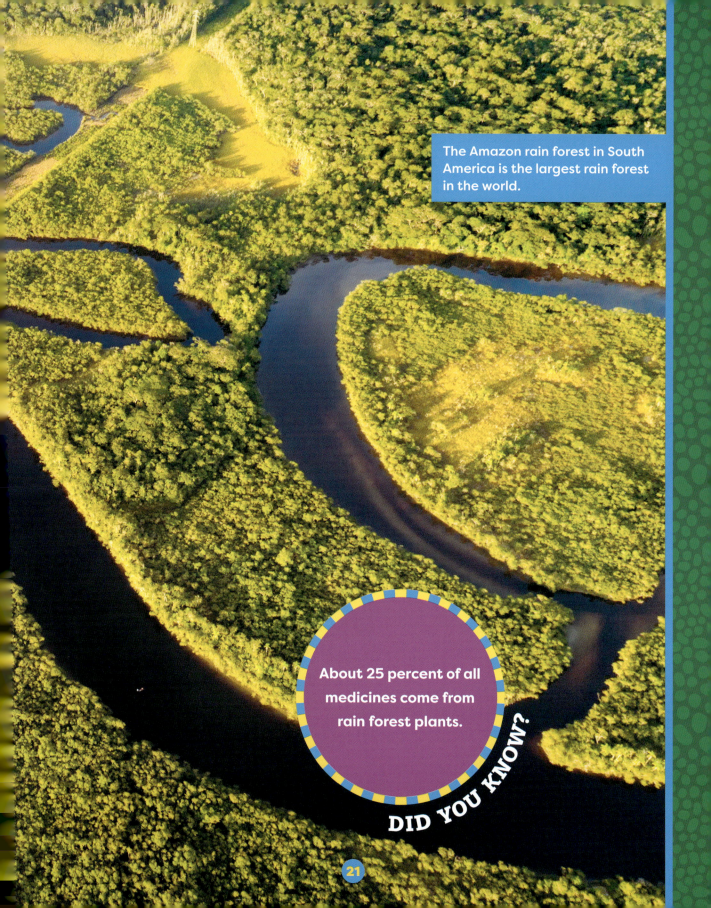

The Amazon rain forest in South America is the largest rain forest in the world.

About 25 percent of all medicines come from rain forest plants.

DID YOU KNOW?

Rain Forest Terrarium

A terrarium is a garden inside a container. It is like a small ecosystem. You can make your own rain forest terrarium.

Materials
- Jar with a lid
- Activated carbon charcoal
- Soil
- Moss
- Tropical plants
- Rocks or twigs
- Spray bottle
- Water

Directions

1. Put a thin layer of activated carbon charcoal in the bottom of your jar.
2. Cover with a layer of potting soil.
3. Plant the tropical plants in the soil.
4. Surround the plants with moss. You can use rocks or twigs to decorate your terrarium.
5. Fill the spray bottle with water. Lightly spray your plants to water them.
6. Close the jar. Your terrarium is now complete!

Glossary

ecosystems (EE-koh-siss-tuhmz) Ecosystems are all of the living and nonliving things in an area. There are many plants and animals in rain forest ecosystems.

equator (ee-KWAY-tur) The equator is an imaginary line around the middle of Earth. The weather is hotter near the equator.

fungi (FUNG-guy) Fungi are a group of living things that look similar to plants but cannot make their own food using sunlight. Fungi grow on the rain forest floor.

nectar (NEK-tuhr) Nectar is a sweet liquid at the bottom of a flower blossom. Hummingbirds drink nectar.

pollinators (PAHL-uh-nayt-urz) Pollinators are animals that carry pollen from one plant to another. Hummingbirds are pollinators.

predators (PREH-duh-turz) Predators are animals that hunt and eat other animals. Green anacondas are predators.

prey (PRAY) Prey are animals that other animals hunt and eat. Flying frogs are prey for some larger animals.

Find Out More

In the Library

Buller, Laura. *Sloths*. New York, NY: DK Publishing, 2019.

Huddleston, Emma. *Looking Into the Rain Forest*. Mankato, MN: The Child's World, 2020.

Youssef, Jagger. *Rainforests*. New York, NY: Gareth Stevens Publishing, 2018.

On the Web

Visit our website for links about rain forests:
childsworld.com/links

Note to Parents, Teachers, and Librarians: We routinely verify our Web links to make sure they are safe and active sites. So encourage your readers to check them out!

Index

algae, 14
equator, 4
fungi, 5, 6
layers, 5

pollinators, 10
predators, 9, 13, 14, 17, 18
prey, 9, 17, 18
temperate rain forest, 4
tropical rain forest, 4, 10